# DAVID
## COPPERFIELD

Written by **Charles Dickens**
Illustrations by **Santiago Calle**

스푼북

# David
# Goes to School

David Copperfield never met his father. He died six months before David was born.

Clara, his mother, missed her husband a lot. She had not been expecting to bring David up alone.

Clara and her son lived in a small village in Suffolk. They were lucky to have a kind and helpful servant-girl in the house.

She was also called Clara, just like David's mother. For this reason, everyone called her by her surname, which was Peggotty.

When David was a few years old, a handsome but rather stern man began to visit the house, to see his mother. His name was Mr Murdstone. David didn't like him very much.

One day, Peggotty told David that she was going to take him to see her brother. She said that he lived in the seaside town of Yarmouth, but they did not stop in the town. Instead, they walked past boatbuilders and ropemakers and soon found themselves by the shore.

'There's my brother's home, Davy,' said Peggotty.

David couldn't see anything except the silver line of the sea in the distance and what looked like a large, upside-down wooden boat.

As they drew nearer to the boat, David saw an iron chimney sticking out of the top of it. Smoke was puffing gently out. The boat also had a neat doorway with a porch and some windows cut in the sides.

Inside it was beautifully clean, snug and warm. David and Peggotty were welcomed by her brother. They stayed in the upside-down boat for two weeks. It was the first holiday David had ever been on. He loved every minute of it.

On the return home, Peggotty put her arm on David's shoulder as they reached the garden gate. She looked nervous.

'Peggotty,' said David. 'What's the matter?'

'Nothing's the matter. Bless you, Master Davy,' she answered.

Why hadn't David's mother come to meet them at the garden gate, as she usually did? David decided to ask.

'Something is the matter, I'm sure,' he said. 'Where's Mama?'

'Well, dear, I really should have told you before now,' said Peggotty.

'Told me what, Peggotty?' said David. He was a little frightened now.

'You have got a pa! A new one. Come and see him.'

'I don't want to see him,' David replied.

But David didn't have a choice. Peggotty took him straight to the sitting room. On one side of the fire sat his mother. On the other side was Mr Murdstone – his new *pa*.

David was not pleased that Edward Murdstone was now his stepfather. There was somehow less space for him in the house now. But at least David was still able to read. Whenever he was unhappy, he would escape inside the pages of a book.

In those days, children often started their education at home.

Mr Murdstone was determined that David should learn things properly. He made David read long pages from his schoolbooks then recite them from memory. If David couldn't, he would pay for it.

Once, David had to memorise a history lesson. Taking his history

book, his mother tested him.

Mr Murdstone sat in a corner,

pretending to read. Really, he was

listening and watching.

First, David mixed up the names

of a couple of dead kings.

Mr Murdstone looked up.

Then David could not recall the

date of a battle.

His mother would have given him the answer if she dared. Instead, she said softly: 'Oh, Davy, Davy!'

'Now, Clara,' said her husband. 'Be firm with the boy. Don't say, "Oh, Davy, Davy!" That's childish. Either he knows his lesson or he does not know it.'

'Davy, try once more, please,' said his mother.

But the more David tried, the more confused he got. His mother mouthed the date at him. Mr

Murdstone spotted her and said in a deep warning voice: 'Clara!'

Mr Murdstone rose from his chair, took the history book from David's mother and threw it at the boy.

Worse was to follow. David failed again and again at these tests. Finally, after another bad lesson, his stepfather decided to beat the knowledge into him.

Mr Murdstone held David's head still with one hand

and raised a cane in the other, ready to hit him. David twisted and caught the hand that was holding him in his mouth. He bit down hard on Mr Murdstone's hand.

Furious, Mr Murdstone hit David even harder. After he had finished beating him, Mr Murdstone locked David up in his room. For five long days, he saw nothing but the walls of his bedroom. He worried about what would happen. David had never hurt anyone before. And he'd certainly never bitten anyone. Was he going to be sent to jail?

On the sixth day, he found out that he would be sent away to school. That was bad enough. Even worse, his mother also believed that David was a wicked boy. Everyone thought it was best that he should leave home.

He was taken by coach to London. There, he was collected by a schoolmaster from Salem House, his new school.

Salem House was a cold, hard place. The headmaster was called Mr Creakle and he loved punishing the boys. He would hit them with a ruler or a cane if they got even the smallest thing wrong.

To add to David's misery, he was made to wear a sign on his back. The sign said: "Look out. He bites".

David Copperfield was being treated like a bad dog. David worried what people might think, but, thankfully, he did make friends at school. He had always liked

reading. At Salem House he retold stories that he'd read at home. The other boys loved to listen.

In time came the terrible news that Clara, David's mother, had died.

When he returned home for the funeral, the only person to comfort him was Peggotty.

But now that Mrs Copperfield was dead, Mr Murdstone got rid of Peggotty. She went to live with her brother in his upside-down boat-house, in Yarmouth.

It seemed Mr Murdstone planned to get rid of David too. Not by sending him back to school, which cost money, but by sending him out to work.

# MEET
# MR MICAWBER

David Copperfield was now
twelve years old. His stepfather
had a business that provided wine
for ships that sailed from the

London docks.
David worked in
the warehouse.
He had to rinse
out the empty
bottles so they
could be reused.

It was dull, lonely work. David thought about the friends he had made at school. Now he was living with a family called the Micawbers. Mr Micawber was a large man with a head as bald and round as an egg. His wife was very thin, and they had four young children.

The Micawbers were very poor
so they were glad to have David as a
paying guest in their shabby house.
Mr Micawber was always waiting
for the family's luck to improve, but
it never did.

Mr Micawber was hopeless at
managing money. But he was kind

to David. He was almost like a
father to him.

One day, the Micawbers decided
to move out of London. They were
going to Plymouth, where Mrs
Micawber came from. They were
hoping that the family's luck would
be better there.

The only friends David had in London were leaving. He still hated washing bottles, so he decided that he would leave the city, too.

David remembered that his real father had an aunt called Betsey Trotwood. Perhaps *she* would take him in if he ran away.

But where did she live?

David wrote a letter to Peggotty. She replied and told him that Miss Betsey lived in Dover.

David set off from London. He didn't have much money. He was forced to sell his waistcoat and then his jacket

on the way to buy some food and drink.
Luckily it was summer, so he could
sleep outside without getting too cold.

After many days of travelling,
David reached Dover. He had to ask
several people where Miss Betsey
Trotwood lived before being directed
to a neat little cottage facing the sea.

As he stood outside the garden gate, David knew what a sight he must look. His shoes had fallen apart after miles of walking. His shirt and trousers were stained with grass and mud from sleeping outdoors. He was covered from head to foot in dust from the roads.

A woman came out of the house. She was wearing gardening gloves and carrying a knife. She noticed David by the gate.

'Go away! No boys here.'

She crouched down to dig up a weed with the knife.

With his heart in his mouth, David crept into the garden. He stood beside her, and touched her with his finger.

'If you please, ma'am–'

She jumped in surprise and looked up.

'If you please, Aunt, I am your great-nephew.'

'Oh Lord!' said Betsey Trotwood.
She sat down on the garden path.

Aunt Betsey may have looked
fierce but she had a kind heart. Even
so, David was worried. His aunt had
written to Mr Murdstone. Now his
stepfather knew where he was!

Sure enough, within a few days, Mr Murdstone arrived at the neat little cottage that faced the sea. His body blocked the front door.

'He disgraced himself by running away from his workplace, Miss Trotwood,' said Mr Murdstone. 'I am here to take him back.'

'And what does the boy say?' said David's aunt. 'Do you want to go back, David?'

David pleaded with Aunt Betsey not to send him back to the bottle-washing warehouse.

'There, you have your answer, Mr Murdstone,' Betsey replied.

Mr Murdstone looked angry. 'Very well, I wash my hands of the boy,' he said, turning and stalking away from the cottage.

# David Goes
# Back to School

Betsey Trotwood adopted David Copperfield. David went to a new school, near Canterbury Cathedral. This was a much better place than Salem House.

While he was at the new school, David lived at Betsey's friend's house. He was a lawyer called Mr Wickfield. The lawyer had a daughter called Agnes, who took care of her father's house. She had

been looking after her father since her mother had died.

The lawyer also had an assistant. He was fifteen years old, and his name was Uriah Heep. He helped Mr Wickfield with everything. He even looked after Aunt Betsey's grey pony when she rode over in her carriage to visit.

David was struck by Uriah's strange looks. He was as thin as a skeleton, with a pinched face and bony arms and legs. The red hair on his head was cut close as stubble.

Uriah often referred to himself as being 'umble – he meant 'humble' – and talked about how good and kind people like Mr Wickfield were to him. But something about the way he talked made David think he was hiding something.

Sometimes Uriah pretended to be impressed by something David said and wrote it down in a little black notebook he carried.

Uriah lived with his mother. He begged David to visit his home for tea. Old Mrs Heep looked like

Uriah. She liked to say she was
'umble, too. But David felt they
were both trying to find out things
about him.

David was glad to leave the
Heeps' 'umble house. As he was
stepping into the street, he was
amazed to hear someone say: 'David
Copperfield! Is it possible?'

It was Mr Micawber.
Now, David was delighted
to see *him*.

The Micawbers
hadn't been lucky
in Plymouth and

now the family were hoping for more luck in Canterbury. They weren't lucky there either and the Micawbers were soon on their way once more. But David was glad see his dear friends again.

The years passed. For the first time in his life, David enjoyed school. He and Agnes Wickfield grew closer, until they were best friends. Agnes told David that she was worried about her father, who seemcd to be drinking too much. She was also afraid that Uriah Heep had too much influence over him.

Her fears were all too true.

# David
# Goes to London

Aunt Betsey suggested that David could become a lawyer. She offered to introduce him to a lawyer in London.

David wasn't sure about this plan, but he didn't have any other ideas and he wanted to please Aunt Betsey.

He started work as a clerk at a firm near St Paul's Cathedral. His aunt was paying for him to

learn this new profession. He lived in a dark little flat at the top of an old house. Agnes Wickfield came to visit him – she was likc a ray of sunshine in his gloomy lodgings.

A much less
welcome visitor
was Uriah Heep.
Uriah said he
was very 'umbled
to be in David's new
home. But he had really come to
talk about the Wickfields.

'Mr Wickfield,' said Uriah, 'has
been very unwise and very careless.'

Uriah pretended to sound sorry
about this but, really, he couldn't
hide how happy he was.

David thought of what Agnes had
said about her father. Mr Wickfield

was a good man but he was quite old and he drank too much.

'Anybody else except a low and 'umble person like me,' continued Uriah, 'would have Mr Wickfield under their thumb by now.'

Uriah Heep reached out his bony hand and pressed down hard on the table with his thumb.

Then he continued, 'Master Copperfield, can I trust you to keep a secret?'

David was afraid of what Uriah was going to say next.

'I have always worshipped the ground Miss Agnes Wickfield walks on,' said Uriah. 'She is very close to her father and I believe one day she'll be close to me. She'll be as 'umble as I am.'

It was plain to David that Uriah was using his influence over Mr Wickfield to get to Agnes. It sounded as though he was planning to marry her. In fact, he already called her 'my Agnes', as if everything was fixed and settled.

David wanted to hit Uriah, but he controlled himself. He simply nodded his head and shook his hand to say goodbye. Uriah's hand was as damp and slimy as a frog's.

# DAVID'S LIFE CHANGES

David's life changed when Betsey Trotwood lost almost all of her money. She said it was because she had made some bad decisions. But David knew that Mr Wickfield advised his aunt about money.

He wondered if it was really Mr Wickfield who had been unwise.

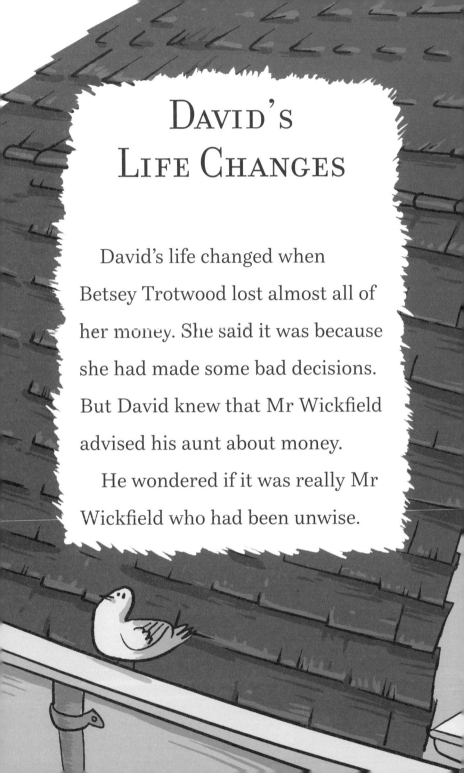

Aunt Betsey was much too kind to blame anyone else for her bad luck. Betsey was forced to leave her little cottage by the sea. She came to share David's flat in London.

He was glad to be able to return some of the kindness that his aunt had shown to him.

Even so, David could not continue working as a lawyer's clerk.

David had always loved reading. Ever since he was a young boy he'd escaped into the pages of a book to avoid his troubles. At Salem House, he'd even made friends by telling them the stories he'd read at home.

Now, David began to write. This time he was not copying other people's words out of legal documents. He was writing for himself. His own words, his own stories. He sent these stories to magazines. Some of them were

published, and David started to
make some money. He only earned
a small amount to begin with. But it
was enough to give him hope for the
future.

Meanwhile, Uriah Heep was worming his way further into Mr Wickfield's law business. Now they were partners: Wickfield and Heep.

Mr Wickfield would always tell David how grateful he was to have

Uriah as a partner. But David heard how dull and flat the old man's voice was when he said this. He noticed too how Uriah encouraged Mr Wickfield to drink more than was good for him. Agnes was powerless to stop Uriah. She saw how her father seemed to be under his spell.

Uriah and his mother moved in to share the Wickfields's house. When David went to visit, he thought they were like two giant vampire bats hanging over the place.

On the other hand, David was happy to see Mr Micawber once again in Canterbury. Luck had finally found them.

The good news was that Mr Micawber was now employed as a clerk in a law firm. The less good news was that he was working for Wickfield and Heep.

Mr Micawber kept his feelings to himself, but David didn't think

his friend liked Uriah Heep at all. In fact, David thought Mr Micawber seemed very unhappy indeed. Mr Micawber couldn't say anything, of course, because he and his family needed the wages that Uriah paid him.

One moonlit evening, David was walking in the countryside just outside Canterbury. He had just published a book, and it was doing very well. People were starting to talk about him.

Uriah caught up with David as he was walking. He squeezed David's hand with his damp, sweaty fingers.

'I am pleased to see you, Master Copperfield,' he began.

David said nothing.

'I am very 'umble at the present moment, Master Copperfield, especially to someone like your good self who has been such a success as a writer.' Uriah paused. 'I am very 'umble at the present moment, but I've got a little power!' he continued.

David knew Uriah was talking about the power he had over Mr Wickfield, Mr Micawber, Agnes, and probably others, too.

David glanced at Uriah's face in the moonlight. It looked like a fox's: sharp and cunning, with glinting eyes.

David knew in that moment that Uriah would never use his power to do good. Uriah would not be happy until he destroyed Mr Wickfield and had Agnes for himself.

# Uriah Heep
# Is Unmasked

David received a letter from
Mr Micawber. It asked David and
his aunt Betsey to meet him in
Canterbury in a few days' time.
The letter spoke of fraud and lies,
and all sorts of horrible things. It
also mentioned Uriah Heep. David
wasn't sure what Mr Micawber
meant,

but it was obvious that his friend
was very upset about something.

David and his aunt arrived
at Wickfield and Heep's office.
Mr Micawber pretended to be
surprised at their arrival.

'Is Mr Wickfield at home?' asked
David.

'He is ill in bed,' said Mr
Micawber, 'but Miss Agnes will be
pleased to see you. I will announce
your arrival to Uriah Heep.'

Mr Micawber could hardly bring himself to say Uriah's name.

He flung open a door to a neighbouring room and announced

in a booming voice: 'Miss Trotwood
and Mr David Copperfield.'

Uriah Heep was writing at a desk.
He was sitting in Mr Wickfield's
chair. He looked up.

'Well,' he said, 'this is indeed an unexpected pleasure.'

Uriah rubbed his bony chin with his hand. He had a suspicious look on his face.

'Things have changed in this office, haven't they, Miss Trotwood, since I was an 'umble clerk, and held your pony?' said Uriah. He made a sickly smile.

'Things may be changed, but you are the same person you always were, Mr Heep,' said Aunt Betsey.

Uriah didn't know what to make of this. Was it a compliment?

Or an insult?

Mr Micawber was standing in the doorway.

'Don't wait, Micawber,' said Uriah.

Mr Micawber didn't move.

'What are you waiting for?' said Uriah impatiently. 'Micawber! Did you hear me tell you *not* to wait?'

'Yes,' replied Mr Micawber, still not moving.

'Then why *do* you wait?' said Uriah.

'Because I choose to wait,' replied Mr. Micawber.

'If you don't do as I say, I'll have to get rid of you,' said Uriah. 'I am your employer, you know, Micawber.'

'No, you are a dishonest man and a villain,' said Mr Micawber.

The words burst out of Mr Micawber. David could tell that he had been itching to say this for a while now.

Uriah rose from Mr Wickfield's seat. He writhed like a snake. By now Agnes Wickfield had appeared.

Mrs Heep entered the room. She was about to speak but Uriah said sharply, 'Hold your tongue, mother. I shall deal with these people.'

Uriah's little eyes darted from David to Aunt Betsey, to Mr Micawber, and finally to Agnes.

Mr Micawber produced several sheets of paper from his pocket.

'Here is a list of your crimes, Heep, you scoundrel–' Uriah made to

grab the papers. But Mr Micawber
snatched up a ruler from the desk
and hit his hand away. It sounded
as if the ruler had fallen on wood.

Mr Micawber read aloud.

'Uriah Heep, I accuse you of deliberately taking advantage of Mr Wickfield when he was tired and confused.'

'Mr Wickfield is a drunken old fool!' said Uriah. All his pretence of being 'umble had gone.

Agnes Wickfield gasped. David put out his arm to comfort her.

Mr Micawber continued: 'You tricked your employer into signing important papers, and pretended they were not important. You claimed money

for the business, and then stole it
yourself.'

'Prove it, you fool,' said Uriah.

'You once had a notebook,
a black notebook, did you not,
Heep?' said Mr Micawber.

David remembered that black notebook. For the first time, Uriah looked alarmed.

'So what if I did have such a notebook, Micawber? It is gone now, burnt to ashes.'

At this, Mr Micawber produced the notebook from another pocket.

'I rescued it from the fireplace in your old house. The notebook is a little battered and burnt, but it's still readable. All your secrets and tricks are written down in here. For instance if I turn to this page–'

Mr Micawber held up the open book and showed it to David, Betsey and Agnes.

'–you will see where this villain Heep has practised copying Mr Wickfield's signature. Again and again, until the forgery is almost perfect. All so he can sign letters and papers in Mr Wickfield's name.

Uriah Heep has been cheating his employer. He has been taking his employer's money. All he has wanted is power!'

By now Agnes was weeping.

Uriah Heep was cornered. He would have slithered from the room if the others hadn't blocked his way.

For the first time Mrs Heep spoke.

'Ury, Ury! Be 'umble, be 'umble. That's the best way.'

'Quiet, mother,' hissed Heep. 'Enough of being 'umble.'

He looked at David and said:

'Copperfield, I have always hated you. You've always been against me.'

'You have always been against the whole world,' replied David.

Much more followed. Uriah Heep would have gone to prison, but instead David and Mr Micawber let him go in exchange for returning all the money and property which he had taken from Mr Wickfield.

It turned out that Uriah had also tricked Aunt Betsey. She had thought it was Mr Wickfield who lost her money.

Being kind-hearted, she had said nothing. But Uriah was behind it all!

With the money returned to her, Aunt Betsey was able to move back into her own house again.

Now Uriah was no longer there to trick him, old Mr Wickfield began to make a slow recovery.

Mr and Mrs Micawber decided to leave England altogether. The family sailed to Australia in the hope that they might finally find luck in that great country.

At last, things went well for the Micawbers. Mr Micawber became a magistrate. He was liked and respected by the people around him.

Things went well for David Copperfield, too. He wrote more and more and became famous.

David was not alone in his success. He and Agnes Wickfield had become far more than best friends – they had grown to love each other. Soon enough they were married. They were very happy together, happier than David had ever expected to be. Now he could give his own children the happy childhood he had wished for as a boy.

# Charles Dickens

Charles Dickens was born in Portsmouth in 1812. Like many of the characters he wrote about, his family were poor and his childhood was difficult. As an adult, he became known around the world for his books. He is remembered as one of the most important writers of his time.

## Santiago Calle

Santiago Calle is an illustrator and animation artist. Born in Medellin, Colombia, he studied at the Edinburgh College of Art in England. Through his experience teaching students, he studied in depth the "sequence art" of comics. In 2006, he set up a studio in Bogota, the capital of Colombia, and is concentrating on producing illustrations, cartoons, and animations.

# DAVID COPPERFIELD

초판 1쇄 발행 2023년 6월 27일

글 찰스 디킨스 | 그림 산티아고 칼레

ISBN 979-11-6581-432-8 (74840)
ISBN 979-11-6581-418-2 (세트)

**발행처** 주식회사 스푼북 | **발행인** 박상희 | **총괄** 김남원
**편집** 김선영·박선정·김선혜·권새미 | **디자인** 조혜진·김광휘 | **마케팅** 손준연·이성호·구혜지
출판신고 2016년 11월 15일 제2017-000267호

주소 (03993) 서울시 마포구 월드컵북로 6길 88-7 ky21빌딩 2층

전화 02-6357-0050(편집) 02-6357-0051(마케팅)

팩스 02-6357-0052 | 전자우편 book@spoonbook.co.kr

**제품명** David Copperfield
**제조자명** 주식회사 스푼북 | **제조국명** 대한민국 | **전화번호** 02-6357-0050
**주소** (03993) 서울시 마포구 월드컵북로6길 88-7 ky21빌딩 2층
**제조년월** 2023년 6월 27일 | **사용연령** 8세 이상
※ KC마크는 이 제품이 공통안전기준에 적합하였음을 의미합니다.

⚠ 주 의

아이들이 모서리에 다치지
않게 주의하세요.